THE URBAN EROTICA
FAIRY TALE COLLECTION

Beau AND

PROFESSOR
Bestialora

I0583735

THE URBAN EROTICA
FAIRY TALE COLLECTION

Beau AND PROFESSOR *Bestialora*

HONEY CUMMINGS

Beau & Professor Bestialora
Copyright © 2020-2024 Honey Cummings. All rights reserved.
Published By: 4 Horsemen Publications, Inc.

4 Horsemen
Publications, Inc.

4 Horsemen Publications, Inc.
PO Box 417
Sylva, NC 28779
4horsemenpublications.com
info@4horsemenpublications.com

Cover & Typesetting by Valerie Willis

Paperback ISBN-13: 978-164450-015-6
Audiobook ISBN-13: 978-164450-014-9
Ebook ISBN-13: 978-164450-013-2

Dedication

To all those looking for one wild moment of sexy fun time with that special someone in your life!

Beau loved books.

He also loved games and anything fantasy including movies and the occasional guilty pleasure of erotic fairy tales. Regardless, this semester had been rough. Stopping in front of Professor Bestialora's office door, he took in a deep breath and held it.

She'd been a monster.

Her temper had been short and he had lost his patience on more than one occasion and the entire class was dismissed the last time. They had fallen into a cold shoulder attitude the last few weeks, and now, she had emailed him to discuss his draft for his final paper. Over the course of the Dark Ages History class, they had been a volatile mix; their opinions on some historical accuracies had shown how passionate they were on the topic.

That was, until she found his profile on YayLove.

They were matches, at a high percentage and considering they were into a lot of the same fandoms, why wouldn't they match? Worse, she sent an inquiry. Beau hadn't responded and soon after, her temper had flared in class. Looking down at his phone, he pulled the profile up and stared at the smile he never once saw in class.

Does she know this is me? She must know. It's the same picture I use for all my university profiles. I mean, the weight of silence between us in class...

And now he stood at her door for their scheduled meeting.

Swallowing, he glared down at his Game of Thrones shirt with disdain. He was a geek and she was, well, his professor for one more week. Clicking off the profile from his phone, he left it still unanswered as he slid the phone in his pocket. Besides, the woman was just on the other side of this door. The words of her profile whispered into his head since he'd read it repeatedly. They had so much in common, but the way things had been since he entered her classroom had been a complete disaster.

Puffing out his cheeks, he knocked, and the door flew open. She didn't look angry. In fact, she looked nervous, scared even.

"Come in, Beau." She waved him in, and the door shut loudly.

The lock slid in place and Beau was now trapped within her castle.

He swallowed down his nerves, "You wanted to see me?"

"You can say that, but..." She walked around and leaned on her desk in front of him, horribly close. "I want an answer."

"Wh-what?" He paled; she couldn't mean ... *that*. "Answer?"

"I know we got off on a bad foot, but after reading your profile on YayLove, I..." She lost

1

her words, a first as her face flushed. "I want to start over, Beau."

"But what about school policy?" Her finger hit his lips, and her own lips tickled Beau's ear.

"Let's not bring school into this. This is about two people looking for sex." Her perfume rolled in his nose, the heat of her body enthralling as her sultry voice whispered. "I've been a bitch. A beast, even. It wasn't my intention, but it's been so long..."

"So long," he echoed as her finger pulled away. "Miss... I mean, Beatrice. I must admit, I didn't think you would have pinged me on YayLove. With how things started, I..."

"I'm sorry." It pained her to say it, but her blue eyes landed on him and something stirred inside him. Her profile echoed, *I love Game of Thrones, D&D, Tolkien, and anything fantasy.* "What is your favorite lovemaking scene in Game of Thrones?"

The question fell from him and caught them both off guard. Her red lips curved upward. Teeth baring, his heart raced, and his cock grew hard. There it was, the smile he had seen on the profile and at last, it was his now, only for him in this private moment. Her long brown locks framed her face like a lion's mane and a hint of her fantasy-loving side emerged as her long, black nails tapped on the desk.

Does she play as a warlock in DnD?

"When Jon Snow finally gave way to his yearning and the wildling girl pounced him at last," she cooed, unbuttoning her jacket, her chest heaving.

His cock rubbed against his jeans and he groaned, watching the jacket slide off her shoulders to reveal hard nipples and a GoT shirt underneath matching his own. Her breasts were large, stretching and distorting the logo of the Stark House. In this moment, he realized the frustration between them hadn't been disdain, but sexual tension. She had figured it out before him, and she intended to act on it in this private moment between them.

He flew from his chair in reckless abandon. Locking lips, he wanted more of Beatrice

Bestialora. His hand slid under her shirt, a moan escaping her as his fingers discovered a braless breast. Her tongue pushed between his lips only to meet his own as he forced her to retreat. He wanted to explore her first, conquer her and stalk her every move.

Pinching her nipple, twisting, she moaned into his mouth. Her fingers were fumbling with his pants and he came to her aid, his freehand quick. His pants fell to the floor. Hot silky fingers grasped his cock, firmly rubbing his length and now he moaned. She circled the tip, slick with pre-cum, then went back to stroking his shaft, her thumb riding the underbelly. His fingers abandoned her breast, unzipping her pencil skirt, feeling hungry to explore more. It fell away revealing black lacy thongs and he pulled away, grinning to admire the view.

"Did you wear these just for me, my little warlock?" She laughed, hiding her face into his shoulder.

Ha! I knew it!

"How did you know what I play in DnD?" Her fingers tightened their grip on his cock, and he groaned.

"I can't decide." He moaned as she stroked his length more aggressively, her breath hot on his neck. "It was... it was either the black fingernails... or..."

"Or what?" Again, her sultry voice in his ear sent chills across his body and he couldn't stop the shudder in his shoulders. "I want to know, my beloved Beau."

"Or how well you're handling my wand."

She laughed and he throbbed in her hand.

Pushing his hand into the front of her underwear, he found the pink valley and flooding river awaiting him. Two fingers fell into the heated depths of her folds and she collapsed into him, her nipples hard against his chest even through his shirt. He stood firm, her grip waning on his throbbing cock; he was winning. Her moans and shivers only encouraged him further, rubbing in and out ever faster. Nails clawed at him through his shirt before balling into fists.

"No more..." Beatrice huffed, her body on fire and rolling on the edge of an orgasm. "I want, I want you."

"You have me." Beau grinned, pulling his fingers out of her pussy, leaving her throbbing with desire.

They both rushed in the break, shirts dropping to the floor and abandoning what little clothes remained. The last of their walls gone, they stood on even playing fields in their completely naked state. With a wave of an arm, Beau sent half the items on her desk clattering to the floor. A Jon Snow Funko doll rolled and stopped to watch them, unmoved by their actions. Beatrice started to scoot her bare ass onto the desk, but Beau gripped her hips. With skill, he twisted her around, pulling her into him.

Hot hands rolled over her bare skin, chills of anticipation traveling across her body as a shudder now rocked her shoulders. One hand glided to her breast, massaging and teasing her nipple. The other rolled over her navel and between her thighs. A finger found her clit and began gliding over it. She stiffened, the sensation only adding to the wetness now dripping down her thighs. A whimper escaped her, and she bit her lip, fighting the orgasm he tempted from her.

She wasn't ready to come, not until he entered her. A wicked grin crossed his face; he could tell she was fighting it, holding it back. He wanted her satisfied again and again. He would make her come for him, against her will. They may have come to a stalemate time and time again in the classroom, but she would no longer be the beast between them here in this moment.

With each moan from her, she could feel his cock throb with delight against her thigh. It excited him to see her lose ground with each passing second. A warm tongue licked across her shoulder and up her neck. Beau began sucking, pulling a hard suction as his hands picked up pace, growing more aggressive with each passing second. Reaching up, she clawed at his hair, failing to pull him from his work on her neck.

"You'll..." A yelp left her lips. Lunging forward only resulted in feeling the muscles in his arms tighten and pull her back. "You'll leave a mark."

Releasing the suction with a large pop of his mouth, he ran a tongue over the hickie.

"Now they'll know I tamed the beast," he cooed, suckling on her earlobe.

Her body shook and he knew she back on the verge of an orgasm. She had fought so hard and it delighted him to feel her body struggle and react against her will. He switched breasts, her thighs tightening over his hand as he shoved his fingers deep inside.

A wail of ecstasy howled from her.

Nails clawed to pull him out from between her legs as she came. Seizing the opportunity, his hands retreated. Pushing her forward, he let her fall onto the cool desk, wiggling and cooing as she rode out the orgasm. She could feel the heat of his hand riding across the small of her back and up her spine. Before she could recover, he slid inside her, his cock hard, throbbing with each squeeze of her pussy. She hadn't finished her orgasm and now fuel had been added to her fire.

Another shriek escaped and he pushed her firmly against the desk, strong fingers wrapped around the back of her neck. He had been slow, pushing inside until he could go no further. Torturous pleasure racked every fiber of her being. He was thick and long, swollen in her tight orgasm. She indulged in the moment of stillness with nothing more than his throbbing cock in response to her squeezing. This was the instant she had wanted and now she had him.

At first, he teased her as he pulled all the way out then pausing before sliding slowly back in, all the way until his hip bones dug into her ass cheeks. Over and over, until her pussy dripped down her thighs. Moaning, he leaned over her and began picking up speed; he was growing closer. His fingers tightened on her neck and hip, their bodies on fire and sprinkled with sweat. She could feel his cock growing harder with each wave. He was nearing his first orgasm and she squeezed her pussy tight.

His hand pulled away from her neck and his body followed, leaving her cold in its wake. Gripping her hips, he spun her around, sliding her far enough on the desk to get the angle he wanted. Arms wrapped around her, arching her back as he entered her again. She whimpered, shuddering as lips wrapped around her nipple. The heat of his lips and the flick of his tongue made her breath catch. His moaning, his thrusting, the very strength of his body sent her over the top once again.

He had made her come again.

Screaming was met with teeth nipping at her nipple. She clung to him, fingernails clawing at the skin of his back. His shoulder blades held her up and his pace quickened. Moaning turned to grunting. The swollen cock tightened against her slick inner walls. Gasping, she gripped the back of his head, tugging his hair and he looked up into her eyes.

"Not there. Cum anywhere you want, but not there." It was a growled plea.

He paused, weighing her blue eyes as he caught his breath. "Anywhere?"

With a toothy smile she echoed, "Anywhere."

She watched his eyes widen; she had opened the doors to allow him a wide range of options. His stare trailed downward across her body as he stood straight. First, his gaze lingered on her lips. He slid out, stroking himself as he prepared his answer. One hand broke free and glided over her breasts, her chest rising and falling, nipples erect with excitement. Once more, his eyes moved back to between her spread legs and he smirked at how swollen and wet he had managed to make her.

Goosebumps trickled across her skin. He hadn't rushed the decision and it filled her with excitement and fear. Instead he savored every detail and option her body had to offer. Her heart raced as his freehand slid over her clit. Fingers dove in and she hummed as he stroked himself, playing with both. He longed to have released there, but she had denied him. Cruel and teasing, just as he had done to her and he looked pained by the options. She tightened around his two fingers as the strokes grew more aggressive in and out of her pussy. He huffed, squeezing and stroking his own cock in frustration.

The fingers left her, sliding downward. Her breath caught in her throat. His eyes watched her face, gauging her reaction. She hadn't revealed anything but want as he slid into her ass. Her secret desire to take all of him, in every way, had moved one step closer without needing to plead. One finger, then two, and she could feel her pussy dripping wet with anticipation. Her body had given him the hint he was hoping for; she wanted him to find this path. Pulling his hand away, he gripped her thighs and pressed the tip of his cock against her anus.

"Anywhere," he repeated, entering just the tip.

She never broke her stare with him. "Anywhere."

He pushed in, the tight fit making both of them moan at the rush of new sensations. Raising her knees, she gave him all the access he needed. He was slow and steady, watching as she arched, grinned how wet she continued to become with each stroke as he built the momentum up once more. Her hand snaked downward, playing with herself, and he found himself on the edge once more, far quicker than he had anticipated. Grunting, slamming himself in and out of her ass, he watched her fingers dive into her pussy as she squealed with another orgasm.

He peaked and she wailed once more.

Vicarious relief washed over him, his cock pushing deep, filling her with cum. He glided his hands over her hips and across her abdomen before squeezing her breasts. Three times she had come for him. She was a beast hungry for sex and he wanted to know how much more could this monstrous appetite could take. How many more times could he make her rise and fall before he won the war in a series of battles?

Breaking away, he squatted between her legs. A thumb circled her clit once and her legs clamped around him like a bear trap. They met his shoulders and he could see her pussy throbbing. With his other hand, he dove into her swollen folds and stroked with uncanny speed. A gasp and shrill filled the room as her fingers gripped his hair, egging him on now that everything had grown oh so sensitive. She tightened and peaked with alarming ease. His cum dribbled from her anus, her entire body tense.

That's four.

Again, he retreated, rubbing her thighs and body down with the heat of his hands. She couldn't speak. Panting, she shuddered as waves of exhilarating sensations jolted through her. He pursed his lips, blowing hot air across her pink valley. Thighs squeezed his broad shoulders, unable to hide the unbearably sensitive parts from their attacker. Deep down, she didn't want it to end.

Knock knock!

"Dr. Bestialora?" It was Professor Gaston from next door. "Are you alright?"

The doorknob jiggled, but it had been locked in preparation of what she had hoped would unfold between Beau and her.

"I'm fi..." She lost the words as silken lips wrapped around her clit and suckled.

"What's going on in there?" Professor Gaston demanded. "Didn't I see Beau come in?"

Beau released her and replied, "We're discussing my work on relationship practices during the Dark Ages and how they differ from the Age of Antiquity."

She gave Beau a skeptical look. "Yes, Beau and I are in the middle of... ah."

Beau's tongue slid across her pussy, hot and silky before sucking on her clit once more. She was sitting up, her hands tangled in his hair and unable to pull him from his prize.

"In the middle... of impor... important discussions for... for next year!" She knew he was making a game of it; could she talk to Gaston and not give herself away? "C-come. Come back later."

There was silence before Professor Gaston pressed, "You sound breathless. Are you unwell?"

"I'm fine!" She shrieked, Beau's work growing more aggressive.

He slid his tongue inside her, making her legs shake. Biting her lip, she fought the urge to squeal or moan. She had been wailing like a banshee; surely, he had heard that. The suckling grew and teeth nipped at her swollen flower. He was devouring her as if she were a melting ice cream cone on a hot summer day. And she didn't want it to stop.

"Please go..." She couldn't tell which man it had been meant for.

"Fine." Professor Gaston sounded pissed off. He knew and yet he continued, "Dinner at my place is still open..."

"No!" She wailed as Beau sucked long and hard on her clit. "I can't stand it. Please, stop!"

Beau let go, flipping her over to grasp the chair so they both face the door. His cock was hard again and he had her teetering on the edge for a fifth time. With Professor Gaston's silhouette in the frosted glass of the door, he wanted her to come knowing someone was there. He wanted Gaston to hear what he couldn't have. He rubbed the tip of his cock against her swollen lips, teasing her, entering her just barely only to pull away and rub his shaft against the wet heat.

"Look, I won't stop."

The doorknob wiggled more, and Beau dipped the tip just barely inside her.

"Stop being a tease." She moaned, abandoning their game.

Beau shushed her, shaking his head as he pulled away and rubbed his hard shaft against her thigh.

"Please give it to me." She whimpered, wiggling her ass against his hips. "I want more."

"You can't have it." He began playing with her clit once more. "I want you to scream it, none of this playing nice or using manners. I can't imagine a warlock being such a pushover."

Her face flushed, her grip on the chair tightening.

"Beatrice? Beau?" She glared at the silhouette as Gaston refused to leave.

"Fuck! Fucking do as I told you, whelp!" Beatrice had abandoned her composure as Beau rammed in her pussy.

His fingers dug into her hips as he fucked her hard and fast; they were peaking together. He started moaning and it was all she needed to roll over the edge a fifth time. Her pussy tightened, holding his cock as he came. She rocked against him, savoring the elations; waves of pleasure made her tremble over and over.

Professor Gaston had walked away at some point in the peaking seconds of pleasure. Beau pulled away, flopping down on her desk behind him. She stayed there, panting, and bent over the chair. Cum dripped from her, mixing with her own wetness, making its way down her legs. Her body remained on fire, riding out the never-ending tide of pleasure.

Beau smirked, catching his breath and enjoying the view.

Maybe I can get her to come a sixth time?

END

Honey Cummings

A passionate, award-winning author of Fantasy, Honey has turned her aim toward erotica. Blending everyday scenarios, and crafting them into steamy, blood-boiling moments for every shade of audience. Whether you want something short and hot, like a student-teacher hook up to the more paranormal flair, where Sleep with Sasquatch has unexpected bonus, look forward to erotic short stories, novellas, and hopefully a Trilogy in the future. Honey's debut erotic short landed at No. 3 in Urban Erotica and continues to satisfy readers time and time again. Be sure to leave her a review and let her know what you think!

Follow Honey Cummings

amazon.com/Honey-Cummings/e/
B07WFX5FDX

AuthorHoneyCummings.com

instagram.com/authorhoneycummings

twitter.com/HoneyCummings2

facebook.com/Author-Honey-
Cummings-101408818012749

MORE HONEY CUMMINGS BOOKS

Sleeping with Sasquatch
Cuddling with
Chupacabra
Naked with New
Jersey Devil
The Erotic Cryptid
Collection

Laying with the
Lady in Blue
Wanton Woman in White
Beating it with
Bloody Mary
The Erotic Ghosts
Collection

Beau and Professor
Bestialora

The Goat's Gruff
Goldie and Her
Three Beards
Pied Piper's Pipe
Princess Pea's Bed
Pinocchio and the
Blow Up Doll
Jack's Beanstalk
Pulling Rapunzel's Hair
The Urban Erotica Fairy
Tale Collection

Curses & Crushes: KU
short story

Queen's Incubus:
YONDER webnovel

WRITING AS VALERIE WILLIS

Cedric: The Demonic Knight

Romasanta: Father of Werewolves

The Oracle: Keeper of the Gaea's Gate

Artemis: Eye of Gaea

King Incubus: A New Reign

Queen Succubus: Holder of the Crown

Val's House of Musings: A Mixed Genre Short Story Collection

Writer's Bane: Research 101

Writer's Bane: Formatting

WRITING MM ROMANCE AS VC WILLIS

The Prince's Priest

The Priest's Assassin

The Assassin's Saint

The Champion's Lord: YONDER webnovel

Champion's Love: KU short story

MORE EROTICA BOOKS FROM 4 HORSEMEN PUBLICATIONS

ALI WHIPPE
Office Hours
Tutoring Center
Athletics
Extra Credit
Financial Aid
Bound for Release
Fetish Circuit
Now You See Me
Sexual Playground
Swingers
Discovered
XTC College Series
Collection

ARIA SKYLAR
Twisted Eros
Seducing Dionysus

CHASTITY VELDT
Molly in Milwaukee
Irene in Indianapolis
Lydia in Louisville
Natasha in Nashville
Alyssa in Atlanta

Betty in Birmingham
Carrie on Campus
Jackie in Jacksonville
A Humorous Erotica
Collection

DALIA LANCE
My Home on
Whore Island
Slumming It on Slut Street
Training of the Tramp
The Imperfect Perfection
Spring Break
72% Match
It Was Meant To Be...
Or Whatever

NICK SAVAGE
The Fairlane Incidents
The Fortunate
Finn Fairlane
The Fragile Finn Fairlane
The Complete Package

LGBT Erotica

DISCOVER MORE AT
4HorsemenPublications.com

www.ingramcontent.com/pod-product-compliance
Lightning Source LLC
Chambersburg PA
CBHW020349110726
47898CB00003B/1101